Military Animals

MILITARY ANIMAL MESSENGERS

by Emma Bassier

DiscoverRoo
An Imprint of Pop!
popbooksonline.com

abdobooks.com

Published by Pop!, a division of ABDO, PO Box 398166, Minneapolis, Minnesota 55439. Copyright ©2022 by Abdo Consulting Group, Inc. International copyrights reserved in all countries. No part of this book may be reproduced in any form without written permission from the publisher. DiscoverRoo™ is a trademark and logo of Pop!.

Printed in the United States of America, North Mankato, Minnesota.

102021
012022

THIS BOOK CONTAINS RECYCLED MATERIALS

Cover Photo: Stevens/Topical Press Agency/Hulton Archive/Getty Images
Interior Photos: Stevens/Topical Press Agency/Hulton Archive/Getty Images, 1; De Luan/Alamy, 5; Berliner Verlag/Archiv/picture-alliance/dpa/AP Images, 6, 13; Shutterstock Images, 7, 20–21; AP Images, 8–9, 12, 14; Gerry Embleton/North Wind Picture Archives, 11; iStockphoto, 16, 27; Defense Visual Information Distribution Service, 17, 22, 25, 28; Library of Congress, 19; Stocktrek Images, Inc./Alamy, 24

Editor: Charly Haley
Series Designer: Laura Graphenteen

Library of Congress Control Number: 2020948838

Publisher's Cataloging-in-Publication Data

Names: Bassier, Emma, author.
Title: Military animal messengers / by Emma Bassier
Description: Minneapolis, Minnesota : Pop!, 2022 | Series: Military animals | Includes online resources and index.
Identifiers: ISBN 9781532169960 (lib. bdg.) | ISBN 9781644945919 (pbk.) | ISBN 9781098240899 (ebook)
Subjects: LCSH: Animals--Juvenile literature. | Working animals--Juvenile literature. | Messengers--Juvenile literature. | Armed Forces--Juvenile literature.
Classification: DDC 355.424--dc23

WELCOME TO DiscoverRoo!

Pop open this book and you'll find QR codes loaded with information, so you can learn even more!

Scan this code* and others like it while you read, or visit the website below to make this book pop!

popbooksonline.com/messengers

*Scanning QR codes requires a web-enabled smart device with a QR code reader app and a camera.

TABLE OF CONTENTS

CHAPTER 1
Crossing a Battlefield............ 4

CHAPTER 2
History.......................... 10

CHAPTER 3
Equipment and Training 18

CHAPTER 4
Messengers Today 26

Making Connections............. 30
Glossary 31
Index........................... 32
Online Resources 32

CROSSING A BATTLEFIELD

Military animal messengers have fought in many wars. One was a dog who worked with the French army in **World War I** (1914–1918).

WATCH A VIDEO HERE!

A World War I soldier stores a message in his dog's collar.

The dog's **handler**, Duval, and other French soldiers were trapped by German soldiers in western France. The French soldiers didn't know how long they could last in the **trenches**.

A military messenger dog leaps over rough terrain during World War I.

Suddenly, Duval's dog appeared sprinting across the battlefield toward him. The Germans fired at the speeding animal. To avoid the bullets, the dog ran in zig-zag patterns. Still, he was shot in the leg and fell. But when Duval called to him, the dog got up and limped the rest of the way to the trench. The message he carried told the French help was coming the next day!

Military messenger dogs must be able to run quickly.

Animals have carried messages for militaries around the world. Dogs and cats have run across battlefields. Pigeons flew with notes strapped to their bodies.

DID YOU KNOW? Message carriers are called couriers. The word *courier* comes from a Latin word meaning "to run."

A French soldier places a carrier pigeon back in its basket during World War II.

CHAPTER 2

HISTORY

Some of the oldest historical records show animals in wars. Horses and dogs worked with people on battlefields. Horses could travel long

DID YOU KNOW? Camels help deliver people, messages, and supplies in deserts.

The earliest American armies used horses to help carry messages.

LEARN MORE HERE!

distances quickly. Sometimes horses delivered messages. But their main purpose was to carry people and supplies.

A US Army pigeon delivered a message from Tunisia to Algeria in 1943. He made the 98-mile (158 km) trip in a little less than two hours.

Pigeons were used to carry messages during wars for more than 5,000 years. Pigeons have a natural homing ability. They can find their way home from thousands of miles away.

Austrian soldiers worked with carrier pigeons in 1915.

A Finnish military dog sits with his handler in 1939. The dog was trained to carry messages.

Dogs were also used as military messengers. They were good at this job because they **bond** with people. Dogs **obey** their **handlers** even during hard tasks.

The first known use of military messenger dogs was in **World War I**. A dog named Taki carried a message in her mouth. The paper was inside a waterproof container.

DID YOU KNOW? Russian soldiers used a cat to deliver messages during World War II (1939–1945).

TIMELINE

3000 BCE
People begin using horses in war. The horses carry messages, people, and supplies.

500 BCE
Pigeon couriers are used in war. The Persian king, Cyrus, sent messages by pigeons to people far away.

1939–1945
During World War II, the number of US military messenger dogs reaches its peak, with more than 10,000 dogs.

1914–1918
During World War I, the number of messenger pigeons reaches its peak. More than 200,000 pigeons are used in the war. Militaries also start using dog messengers.

2019
The US military has 2,300 dogs, though most are no longer used as messengers. Technology has replaced most animal messengers.

CHAPTER 3
EQUIPMENT AND TRAINING

When soldiers traveled to different battlefields in the 1900s, they brought pigeons. They kept the birds in cages. Soldiers attached messages to pigeons. Then the birds flew home

COMPLETE AN ACTIVITY HERE!

Japanese soldiers release carrier pigeons from their cages.

to headquarters. The messages often told leaders what happened in battles or asked for supplies.

People attach tags to pigeons' legs to keep track of them.

Notes can be tied to a pigeon's neck or leg with a string. Or a pigeon can wear a **harness** that holds notes. Military pigeons only carry messages. They don't need special training.

DID YOU KNOW? During World War II, a pigeon named Gustav flew more than 150 miles (241 km) in one day to deliver a message.

US military dogs and their handlers train together, including on obstacle courses.

Military dogs are trained to carry messages and much more. **Handlers** train alongside their dogs.

US military dogs start training when they are 18 to 24 months old. Their first training program is 120 days long. Then they usually have more training before going on a **mission**.

A STRONG BOND

Each dog and its handler develop a very close relationship. This relationship starts with training. The handler teaches the dog commands such as sit and stay. Many dogs learn best when they are rewarded. So after practicing a task correctly, they get to play.

Military dogs often wear vests. Notes can be tucked into pockets on the vest.

Small cameras are built into some dog vests. They let people see videos of where the dogs go. The videos are like messages.

A military working dog sits with his gear.

MILITARY DOG GEAR

Gear for military dogs is improving. The dogs can wear different gear for different tasks. They may wear goggles to protect their eyes. They may wear ear protection too.

CHAPTER 4

MESSENGERS TODAY

Today most military messages can be sent with technology. Radios and computers can instantly send messages around the world. But some armies still use animals to deliver messages.

LEARN MORE HERE!

Computers, tablets, and other technology have replaced a lot of military animal messengers.

27

Military members take care of their animals.

> **DID YOU KNOW?** Dogs can sniff out dangerous weapons and check if an area is safe for soldiers.

Many animals have worked for militaries. Pigeons delivered messages from the battlefield to home. Dogs are useful for many military tasks. They can deliver messages. Military animal messengers have helped people communicate for many years.

MAKING CONNECTIONS

TEXT-TO-SELF

Would you trust an animal to carry a message for you? Why or why not?

TEXT-TO-TEXT

Have you read other books about military animals? How were those animals similar to or different from the ones described in this book?

TEXT-TO-WORLD

Animals help people do many tasks. Besides helping in the military, what else can animals do to make people's lives easier or better?

GLOSSARY

bond — to form a strong, emotional relationship with another.

handler — a person who is in charge of a military animal.

harness — a vest or strap that wraps tightly to an animal's body.

mission — a military assignment.

obey — to follow rules or do what a person says.

trench — a deep, narrow pit that many soldiers fought from and hid in during World War I.

World War I — occurring from 1914 to 1918 and fought in Europe. Great Britain, France, Russia, the United States, and their allies were on one side. Germany, Austria-Hungary, and their allies were on the other side.

INDEX

cats, 8, 15
computers, 26

dogs, 4–8, 10, 15, 17, 23–24, 25, 29

handlers, 5, 15, 23
homing, 12
horses, 10–11, 16

pigeons, 8, 12, 16, 17, 18, 21, 29

training, 21, 23

World War I, 4, 15, 17
World War II, 15, 17, 21

ONLINE RESOURCES
popbooksonline.com

Scan this code* and others like it while you read, or visit the website below to make this book pop!

popbooksonline.com/messengers

*Scanning QR codes requires a web-enabled smart device with a QR code reader app and a camera.